The Story
of the Other
Wise Man

HENRY VAN DYKE

The Story of the Other Wise Man

HODDER AND STOUGHTON
London Sydney Auckland Toronto

Van Dyke, Henry L, b.1852
  The story of the other Wise Man.
  I. Title
  823'.9'1F   PS3116.S/

  ISBN 0 340 23412 1

First published in this edition 1978

This edition completely reset,
and with specially drawn illustrations by
Derek Lucas and designed by Drummond Chapman:
Copyright © 1978 by Hodder & Stoughton Limited.

Photoset and printed in Great Britain for
Hodder and Stoughton Limited,
Mill Road, Dunton Green, Sevenoaks, Kent,
by Lowe & Brydone Printers Limited,
Thetford, Norfolk.

Contents

Dedication

This edition is specially dedicated
to the boys, past and present, of
Marlborough House School, Hawkhurst,
Kent, who have been inspired by
Henry Van Dyke's fable.

*I*t is now some years since this little story was set afloat on the sea of books. It is not a man-of-war, nor even a high-sided merchantman; only a small, peaceful sailing-vessel. Yet it has had rather an adventurous voyage. Twice it has fallen into the hands of pirates. The tides have carried it to far countries. It has been passed through the translator's port of entry into German, French, Armenian, Turkish, and perhaps some other foreign regions. Once I caught sight of it flying the outlandish flag of a brand-new phonetic language along the coasts of France; and once it was claimed by a dealer in antiquities as a long-lost legend of the Orient. Best of all, it has slipped quietly into many a far-away harbour that I have never seen, and found a

Preface

kindly welcome, and brought back messages of good cheer from unknown friends.

Now it has turned home to be new-rigged and fitted for further voyaging. Before it is sent out again I have been asked to tell where the story came from and what it means.

I do not know where it came from—out of the air, perhaps. One thing is certain, it is not written in any other book, nor is it to be found among the ancient lore of the East. And yet I have never felt as if it were my own. It was a gift. It was sent to me; and it seemed as if I knew the Giver, though His name was not spoken.

The year had been full of sickness and sorrow. Every day brought trouble. Every night was tormented with pain. They are very long—those nights when one lies awake, and hears the labouring heart pumping wearily at its task, and watches for the morning, not knowing whether it will ever dawn. They are not nights of fear; for the thought of death grows strangely familiar when you have lived with it for a year. Besides, after a time you come to feel like a soldier who has been long standing still under fire; any change would be a relief. But they are lonely nights; they are very heavy nights. And their heaviest burden is this:

You must face the thought that your work in the world may be almost ended, but you know that it is not nearly finished.

You have not solved the problems that perplexed you. You have not reached the goal that you aimed at. You have not accomplished the great task that you set for yourself. You are still on the way; and perhaps your journey must end now — nowhere — in the dark.

Well, it was in one of these long, lonely nights that this story came to me. I had studied and loved the curious tales of the Three Wise Men of the East as they are told in the *Golden Legend* of Jacobus de Voragine and other mediæval books. But of the Fourth Wise Man I had never heard until that night. Then I saw him distinctly, moving through the shadows in a little circle of light. His countenance was as clear as the memory of my father's face as I saw it for the last time a few months before. The narrative of his journeyings and trials and disappointments ran without a break. Even certain sentences came to me complete and unforgettable, clear-cut like a cameo. All that I had to do was to follow Artaban, step by step, as the tale went on, from the beginning to the end of his pilgrimage.

Perhaps this may explain some things in the story. I have been asked many times why I made the Fourth Wise Man tell a lie, in the cottage at Bethlehem, to save the little child's life.

I did not make him tell a lie.

What Artaban said to the soldiers he said for himself, because he could not help it.

Is a lie ever justifiable? Perhaps not. But may it not sometimes seem inevitable?

And if it were a sin, might not a man confess it, and be pardoned for it more easily than for the greater sin of spiritual selfishness, or indifference, or the betrayal of innocent blood? That is what I saw Artaban do. That is what I heard him say. All through his life he was trying to do the best that he could. It was not perfect. But there are some kinds of failure that are better than success.

Though the story of the Fourth Wise Man came to me suddenly and without labour, there was a great deal of study and toil to be done before it could be written down. An idea arrives without effort; a form can only be wrought out by patient labour. If your story is worth telling, you ought to love it enough to be willing to work over it until it is true—true not only to the ideal, but true also to the real. The light is a gift;

but the local colour can only be seen by one who looks for it long and steadily. Artaban went with me while I toiled through a score of volumes of ancient history and travel. I saw his figure while I journeyed on the motionless sea of the desert and in the strange cities of the East.

And now that his story is told, what does it mean?

How can I tell? What does life mean? If the meaning could be put into a sentence there would be no need of telling the story.

1895   HENRY VAN DYKE.

You know the story of the Three Wise Men of the East, and how they travelled from far away to offer their gifts at the manger-cradle in Bethlehem. But have you ever heard the story of the Other Wise Man, who also saw the star in its rising, and set out to follow it, yet did not arrive with his brethren in the presence of the young child Jesus?

Of the great desire of
this fourth pilgrim, and how
it was denied, yet accomplished
in the denial; of his many wanderings
and the probations of his soul;
of the long way of his seeking,
and the strange way of his finding,
the One whom he sought—I would
tell the tale as I have heard
fragments of it in the Hall of
Dreams, in the palace of
the Heart of Man.

Who seeks for heaven alone
to save his soul
May keep the path, but will
not reach the goal;
While he who walks in love
may wander far,
Yet God will bring him
where the blessed are.

The
Sign
in the
Sky

*O*n the days when Augustus Cæsar was master of many kings and Herod reigned in Jerusalem, there lived in the city of Ecbatana, among the mountains of Persia, a certain man named Artaban, the Median. His house stood close to the outermost of the seven walls which encircled the royal treasury. From his roof he could look over the rising battlements of black and white and crimson and blue and red and silver and gold, to the hill where the summer palace of the Parthian emperors glittered like a jewel in a sevenfold crown.

Around the dwelling of Artaban spread a fair garden, a tangle of flowers and fruit trees, watered by a score of streams descending from the slopes of Mount Orontes, and made musical by innumerable birds. But all colour was lost in the soft

18

and odorous darkness of the late September night, and all sounds were hushed in the deep charm of its silence, save the splashing of the water, like a voice half sobbing and half laughing under the shadows. High above the trees a dim glow of light shone through the curtained arches of the upper chamber, where the master of the house was holding council with his friends.

He stood by the doorway to greet his guests—a tall, dark man of about forty years, with brilliant eyes set near-together under his broad brow, and firm lines graven around his fine, thin lips; the brow of a dreamer and the mouth of a soldier, a man of sensitive feeling but inflexible will—one of those who, in whatever age they may live, are born for inward conflict and a life of quest.

His robe was of pure white wool
thrown over a tunic of silk; and a
white, pointed cap, with long lapel
at the sides, rested on his flowing
black hair. It was the dress of the
ancient priesthood of the Magi
called the fire-worshippers.

"Welcome!" he said, in his low
pleasant voice, as one after another
entered the room—"welcome, Ab-
dus; peace be with you, Rhodaspe
and Tigranes, and with you my
father, Abgarus. You are all welcome, and this house grows bright
with the joy of your presence."

There were nine of the men, dif-
fering widely in age, but alike in
the richness of their dress of many-
coloured silks, and in the massive
golden collars around their necks
marking them as Parthian nobles,
and in the winged circles of gold
resting upon their breasts, the sign

of the followers of Zoroaster.

They took their places around a small black altar at the end of the room, where a tiny flame was burning. Artaban, standing beside it, and waving a barsom of thin tamarisk branches above the fire, fed it with dry sticks of pine and fragrant oils. Then he began the ancient chant of the Yasna, and the voices of his companions joined in the beautiful hymn to Ahura-Mazda:

We worship the Spirit Divine,
  all wisdom and goodness possessing,
Surrounded by Holy Immortals,
    the givers of bounty and blessing,
We joy in the works of His hands,
  His truth and His power confessing.

We praise all the things that are pure,
      for these are His only Creation;
The thoughts that are true, and the words
  and deeds that have won approbation;
These are supported by Him
    and for these we make adoration.

The Sign in the Sky

Hear us, O Mazda! Thou livest
    in truth and in heavenly gladness;
Cleanse us from falsehood, and keep us
    from evil and bondage to badness;
Pour out the light and the joy of Thy life
    on our darkness and sadness.

Shine on our gardens and fields,
    Shine on our working and weaving;
Shine on the whole race of man,
    Believing and unbelieving;
    Shine on us now through the night,
    Shine on us now in Thy might,
The flame of our holy love
and the song of our worship receiving.

The fire rose with the chant, throbbing as if it were made of musical flame, until it cast a bright illumination through the whole apartment, revealing its simplicity and splendour.

The floor was laid with tiles of dark blue veined with white; pilasters of twisted silver stood out against the blue walls; the clear-story of round-arched windows above them was hung with azure silk; the vaulted ceiling was a pavement of sapphires, like the body of heaven in its clearness, sown with silver stars. From the four corners of the roof hung four golden magic-wheels, called the tongues of the gods. At the eastern end, behind the altar, there were two dark-red pillars of porphyry; above them a lintel of the same stone, on which was carved the figure of a winged archer, with his arrow set to the string and his bow drawn.

The doorway between the pillars, which opened upon the terrace of the roof, was covered with a heavy curtain of the colour of a ripe pomegranate, embroidered with innumerable golden rays shooting upward from the floor.

In effect the room was like a quiet, starry night, all azure and silver, flushed in the east with rosy promise of the dawn. It was, as the house of a man should be, an expression of the character and spirit of the master.

He turned to his friends when the song was ended, and invited them to be seated on the divan at the western end of the room.

"You have come to-night," said he, looking around the circle, "at my call, as the faithful scholars of Zoroaster, to renew your worship and rekindle your faith in the God of Purity, even as this fire has been rekindled on the altar. We worship not the fire, but Him of whom it is the chosen symbol, because it is the purest of all created things. It speaks to us of one who is Light and Truth. Is it not so, my father?"

"It is well said, my son," answered the venerable Abgarus. "The enlightened are never idolaters. They lift the veil of the form and go in to the shrine of the reality, and new light and truth are coming to them continually through the old symbols."

"Hear me, then, my father and my friends," said Artaban, very quietly, "while I tell you of the new light and truth that have come to me through the most ancient of all signs. We have searched the secrets of nature together, and studied the healing virtues of water and fire and the plants. We have read also the books of prophecy in which the future is dimly foretold in words that are hard to understand. But the highest of all learning is the knowledge of the stars. To trace

their courses is to untangle the
threads of the mystery of life from
the beginning to the end. If we
could follow them perfectly, nothing would be hidden from us. But
is not our knowledge of them still
incomplete? Are there not many
stars still beyond our horizon—
lights that are known only to the
dwellers in the far south-land,
among the spice-trees of Punt and
the gold-mines of Ophir?"

There was a murmur of assent
among the listeners.

"The stars," said Tigranes, "are
the thoughts of the Eternal. They
are numberless. But the thoughts
of man can be counted, like the
years of his life. The wisdom of
the Magi is the greatest of all wis-
doms on earth, because it knows
its own ignorance. And that is
the secret of power. We keep men

always looking and waiting for a new sunrise. But we ourselves know that the darkness is equal to the light, and that the conflict between them will never be ended."

"That does not satisfy me," answered Artaban, "for, if the waiting must be endless, if there could be no fulfilment of it, then it would not be wisdom to look and wait. We should become like those new teachers of the Greeks, who say that there is no truth, and that the only wise men are those who spend their lives in discovering and exposing the lies that have been believed in the world. But the new sunrise will certainly dawn in the appointed time. Do not our own books tell us that this will come to pass, and that men will see the brightness of a great light?"

"That is true," said the voice of Abgarus; "every faithful disciple of Zoroaster knows the prophecy of the Avesta and carries the word in his heart. 'In that day Sosiosh the Victorious shall arise out of the number of the prophets in the east country. Around him shall shine a mighty brightness, and he shall make life everlasting, incorruptible, and immortal, and the dead shall rise again.' "

"This is a dark saying," said Tigranes, "and it may be that we shall never understand it. It is better to consider the things that are near at hand, and to increase the influence of the Magi in their own country, rather than to look for one who may be a stranger, and to whom we must resign our power."

The others seemed to approve

these words. There was a silent feel-ling of agreement manifest among them; their looks responded with that indefinable expression which always follows when a speaker has uttered the thought that has been slumbering in the hearts of his listeners. But Artaban turned to Abgarus with a glow in his face, and said:

"My father, I have kept this prophecy in the secret place of my soul. Religion without a great hope would be like an altar with-out a living fire. And now the flame has burned more brightly, and by the light of it I have read other words which also have come from the fountain of Truth, and speak yet more clearly of the ris-ing of the Victorious One in his brightness."

He drew from the breast of his

tunic two small rolls of fine linen, with writing upon them, and unfolded them carefully upon his knee.

"In the years that are lost in the past, long before our fathers came into the land of Babylon, there were wise men in Chaldea, from whom the first of the Magi learned the secret of the heavens. And of these Balaam, the son of Beor, was one of the mightiest. Hear the words of his prophecy: 'There shall come a star out of Jacob, and a sceptre shall arise out of Israel.' "

The lips of Tigranes drew downward with contempt, as he said:

"Judah was a captive by the waters of Babylon, and the sons of Jacob were in bondage to our kings. The tribes of Israel are scattered through the mountains like lost sheep, and from the remnant that dwells in Judea under the yoke of Rome neither star nor sceptre shall arise."

"And yet," answered Artaban, "it was the Hebrew Daniel, the mighty searcher of dreams, the counsellor of kings, the wise Belteshazzar, who was most honoured and beloved of our great King Cyrus. A prophet of sure things and a reader of the thoughts of God, Daniel proved himself to our people. And these are the words that he wrote." (Artaban read from the second roll:) " 'Know, therefore, and understand that from the going forth of the commandment to restore Jerusalem unto the Anointed One, the Prince, the time shall be seven and three-score and two weeks.' "

"But, my son," said Abgarus,

doubtfully, "these are mystical numbers. Who can interpret them, or who can find the key that shall unlock their meaning?"

Artaban answered: "It has been shown to me and to my three companions among the Magi—Caspar, Melchior, and Balthazar. We have searched the ancient tablets of Chaldea and computed the time. It falls in this year. We have studied the sky, and in the spring of the year we saw two of the greatest stars draw near together in the sign of the Fish, which is the house of the Hebrews. We also saw a new star there, which shone for one night and then vanished. Now again the two great planets are meeting. This night is their conjunction. My three brothers are watching at the ancient Temple of the Seven Spheres, at Borsippa, in Babylonia, and I am watching here. If the star shines again, they will wait ten days for me at the temple, and then we will set out together for Jerusalem, to see and worship the promised one who shall be born King of Israel. I believe the sign will come. I have made ready for the journey. I have sold my house and my possessions, and bought these three jewels—a sapphire, a ruby, and a pearl—to carry them as tribute to the King. And I ask you to go with me on the pilgrimage, that we may have joy together in finding the Prince who is worthy to be served."

While he was speaking he thrust his hand into the inmost fold of his girdle and drew out three great gems—one blue as a fragment of the night sky, one redder than a ray of sunrise, and one as pure as the peak of a snow mountain at twilight—and laid them on the outspread linen scrolls before him.

But his friends looked on with strange and alien eyes. A veil of doubt and mistrust came over their faces, like a fog creeping up from the marshes to hide the hills. They glanced at each other with looks of wonder and pity, as those who have listened to incredible sayings, the story of a wild vision, or the proposal of an impossible enterprise.

At last Tigranes said: "Artaban, this is a vain dream. It comes from too much looking upon the stars and the cherishing of lofty thoughts. It would be wiser to spend the time in gathering money for the new fire-temple at Chala. No king will ever rise from the

broken race of Israel, and no end will ever come to the eternal strife of light and darkness. He who looks for it is a chaser of shadows. Farewell."

And another said: "Artaban, I have no knowledge of these things, and my office as guardian of the royal treasure binds me here. The quest is not for me. But if thou must follow it, fare thee well."

And another said: "In my house there sleeps a new bride, and I cannot leave her nor take her with me on this strange journey. This quest is not for me. But may thy steps be prospered wherever thou goest. So, farewell."

And another said: "I am ill and unfit for hardship, but there is a man among my servants whom I will send with thee when thou goest, to bring me word how thou farest."

But Abgarus, the oldest and the one who loved Artaban the best, lingered after the others had gone, and said, gravely: "My son, it may be that the light of truth is in this sign that has appeared in the skies, and then it will surely lead to the Prince and the mighty brightness. Or it may be that it is only a shadow of the light, as Tigranes has said, and then he who follows it will have only a long pilgrimage and an empty search. But it is better to follow even the shadow of the best than to remain content with the worst. And those who would see wonderful things must often be ready to travel alone. I am too old for this journey, but my heart shall be a companion of the pilgrimage day and night, and

I shall know the end of thy quest. Go in peace."

So one by one they went out of the azure chamber with its silver stars, and Artaban was left in solitude.

He gathered up the jewels and replaced them in his girdle. For a long time he stood and watched the flame that flickered and sank upon the altar. Then he crossed the hall, lifted the heavy curtain, and passed out between the dull red pillars of porphyry to the terrace on the roof.

The shiver that thrills through the earth ere she rouses from her night sleep had already begun, and the cool wind that heralds the daybreak was drawing downward from the lofty, snow-traced ravines of Mount Orontes. Birds, half awakened, crept and chirped among the rustling leaves, and the smell of ripened grapes came in brief wafts from the arbours.

Far over the eastern plain a white mist stretched like a lake. But where the distant peak of Zagros serrated the western horizon the sky was clear. Jupiter and Saturn rolled together like drops of lambent flame about to blend in one.

As Artaban watched them, behold, an azure spark was born out of the darkness beneath, rounding itself with purple splendours to a crimson sphere, and spiring upward through rays of saffron and orange into a point of white radiance. Tiny and infinitely remote, yet perfect in every part, it pulsated in the enormous vault as if the three jewels in the Magian's breast had mingled and been trans-

The Sign in the Sky

formed into a living heart of light.

He bowed his head. He covered his brow with his hands.

"It is the sign," he said. "The King is coming, and I will go to meet him."

By the
Waters
of
Babylon

*A*ll night long Vasda, the swiftest of Artaban's horses, had been waiting, saddled and bridled, in her stall, pawing the ground impatiently, and shaking her bit as if she shared the eagerness of her master's purpose, though she knew not its meaning.

Before the birds had fully roused to their strong, high, joyful chant of morning song, before the white mist had begun to lift lazily from the plain, the other wise man was in the saddle, riding swiftly along the high-road, which skirted the base of Mount Orontes, westward.

How close, how intimate is the comradeship between a man and his favourite horse on a long journey. It is a silent, comprehensive friendship, an intercourse beyond the need of words.

They drink at the same wayside springs, and sleep under the same guardian stars. They are conscious together of the subduing spell of nightfall and the quickening joy of daybreak. The master shares his evening meal with his hungry companion, and feels the soft, moist lips caressing the palm of his hand as they close over the morsel of bread. In the grey dawn he is roused from his bivouac by the gentle stir of a warm, sweet breath over his sleeping face, and looks up into the eyes of his faithful fellow-traveller, ready and waiting for the toil of the day. Surely, unless he is a pagan and an unbeliever, by whatever name he calls upon his God, he will thank Him for this voiceless sympathy, this dumb affection, and his morning prayer will embrace a double blessing—God bless us

both, and keep our feet from falling
and our souls from death!

And then, through the keen
morning air, the swift hoofs beat
their spirited music along the road,
keeping time to the pulsing of two
hearts that are moved with the
same eager desire—to conquer
space, to devour the distance, to
attain the goal of the journey.

Artaban must indeed ride wisely
and well if he would keep the
appointed hour with the other
Magi; for the route was a hundred
and fifty parasangs, and fifteen was
the utmost that he could travel
in a day. But he knew Vasda's
strength, and pushed forward without anxiety, making the fixed distance every day, though he must
travel late into the night, and in
the morning long before sunrise.

He passed along the brown

slopes of Mount Orontes, furrowed by the rocky courses of a hundred torrents.

He crossed the level plains of
the Nisæans, where the famous
herds of horses, feeding in the
wide pastures, tossed their heads
at Vasda's approach, and galloped
away with a thunder of many
hoofs, and flocks of wild birds rose
suddenly from the swampy meadows, wheeling in great circles with
a shining flutter of innumerable
wings and shrill cries of surprise.

He traversed the fertile fields of
Concabar, where the dust from the
threshing-floors filled the air with
a golden mist, half hiding the huge
temple of Astarte with its four-
hundred pillars.

At Baghistan, among the rich
gardens watered by fountains from
the rock, he looked up at the

mountain thrusting its immense
rugged brow out over the road,
and saw the figure of King Darius
trampling upon his fallen foes, and
the proud list of his wars and con-
quests graven high upon the face
of the eternal cliff.

Over many a cold and desolate
pass, crawling painfully across the
wind-swept shoulders of the hills;
down many a black mountain-
gorge, where the river roared and
raced before him like a savage
guide; across many a smiling vale,
with terraces of yellow limestone
full of vines and fruit trees;
through the oak groves of Carine
and the dark Gates of Zagros,
walled in by precipices; into the
ancient city of Chala, where the
people of Samaria had been kept
in captivity long ago; and out
again by the mighty portal, riven

through the encircling hills, where he saw the image of the High Priest of the Magi sculptured on the wall of rock, with hand up-lifted as if to bless the centuries of pilgrims; past the entrance of the narrow defile, filled from end to end with orchards of peaches and figs, through which the river Gyndes foamed down to meet him; over the broad rice-fields where the autumnal vapours spread their deathly mists; following along the course of the river, under tremulous shadows of poplar and tamarind, among the lower hills; and out upon the flat plain, where the road ran straight as an arrow through the stubble-fields and parched meadows; past the city of Ctesiphon, where the Parthian emperors reigned and the vast metropolis of Seleucia which Alex-

ander built; across the swirling
floods of Tigris and the many
channels of Euphrates, flowing
yellow through the corn-lands—
Artaban pressed onward until he
arrived, at nightfall of the tenth
day, beneath the shattered walls
of populous Babylon.

Vasda was almost spent, and he
would gladly have turned into the
city to find rest and refreshment for
himself and for her. But he knew
that it was three hours' journey
yet to the Temple of the Seven
Spheres, and he must reach the
place by midnight if he would find
his comrades waiting. So he did
not halt, but rode steadily across
the stubble-fields.

A grove of date-palms made
an island of gloom in the pale yellow sea. As she passed into the
shadow Vasda slackened her pace,

and began to pick her way more carefully.

Near the farther end of the darkness an access of caution seemed to fall upon her. She scented some danger or difficulty; it was not in her heart to fly from it—only to be prepared for it, and to meet it wisely, as a good horse should do. The grove was close and silent as the tomb; not a leaf rustled, not a bird sang.

She felt her steps before her delicately, carrying her head low, and sighing now and then with apprehension. At last she gave a quick breath of anxiety and dismay, and stood stock-still, quivering in every muscle, before a dark object in the shadow of the last palm-tree.

Artaban dismounted. The dim starlight revealed the form of a man lying across the road. His humble dress and the outline of his haggard face showed that he was probably one of the poor Hebrew exiles who still dwelt in great numbers in the vicinity. His pallid skin, dry and yellow as parchment, bore the mark of the deadly fever which ravaged the marsh-lands in autumn. The chill of death was in his lean hand, and as Artaban released it the arm fell back inertly upon the motionless breast.

He turned away with a thought of pity, consigning the body to that strange burial which the Magians deemed most fitting—the funeral of the desert, from which the kites and vultures rise on dark wings, and the beasts of prey slink furtively away, leaving only a heap of white bones in the sand.

But, as he turned, a long, faint,

ghostly sigh came from the man's
lips. The brown, bony fingers clo-
sed convulsively on the hem of the
Magian's robe and held him fast.

Artaban's heart leaped to his
throat, not with fear, but with a
dumb resentment at the impor-
tunity of this blind delay.

How could he stay here in the
darkness to minister to a dying
stranger? What claim had this
unknown fragment of human life
upon his compassion or his service?
If he lingered but for an hour he
could hardly reach Borsippa at
the appointed time. His companions would think he had given
up the journey. They would go
without him. He would lose his
quest.

But if he went on now, the man
would surely die. If he stayed,
life might be restored. His spirit

throbbed and fluttered with the urgency of the crisis. Should he risk the great reward of his divine faith for the sake of a single deed of human love? Should he turn aside, if only for a moment, from the following of the star, to give a cup of cold water to a poor, perishing Hebrew?

"God of truth and purity," he prayed, "direct me in the holy path, the way of wisdom which Thou only knowest."

Then he turned back to the sick man. Loosening the grasp of his hand, he carried him to a little mound at the foot of the palm-tree.

He unbound the thick folds of the turban and opened the garment above the sunken breast. He brought water from one of the small canals nearby, and moistened the sufferer's brow and mouth.

He mingled a draught of one of those simple but potent remedies which he carried always in his girdle—for the Magians were physicians as well as astrologers—and poured it slowly between the colourless lips. Hour after hour he laboured as only a skilful healer of disease can do; and at last the man's strength returned; he sat up and looked about him.

"Who art thou?" he said, in the rude dialect of the country, "and why hast thou sought me here to bring back my life?"

"I am Artaban the Magian, of the city of Ecbatana, and I am going to Jerusalem in search of one who is to be born King of the Jews, a great Prince and Deliverer of all men. I dare not delay any longer upon my journey, for the caravan that has waited for me may depart

without me. But see, here is all
that I have left of bread and wine,
and here is a potion of healing
herbs. When thy strength is restored thou canst find the dwell-
ings of the Hebrews among the
houses of Babylon."

The Jew raised his trembling
hand solemnly to heaven.

"Now may the God of Abraham
and Isaac and Jacob bless and
prosper the journey of the merciful, and bring him in peace to his
desired haven. But stay; I have
nothing to give thee in return—
only this: that I can tell thee
where the Messiah must be sought.
For our prophets have said that
he should be born not in Jerusalem, but in Bethlehem of Judah.
May the Lord bring thee in safety
to that place, because thou hast
had pity upon the sick."

It was already long past midnight. Artaban rode in haste, and Vasda, restored by the brief rest, ran eagerly through the silent plain and swam the channels of the river. She put forth the remnant of her strength, and fled over the ground like a gazelle.

But the first beam of the sun sent her shadow before her as she entered upon the final stadium of the journey, and the eyes of Artaban, anxiously scanning the great mound of Nimrod and the Temple of the Seven Spheres, could discern no trace of his friends.

The many-coloured terraces of black and orange and red and yellow and green and blue and white, shattered by the convulsions of nature, and crumbling under the repeated blows of human violence, still glittered like a ruined rainbow in the morning light.

Artaban rode swiftly around the hill. He dismounted and climbed to the highest terrace, looking out toward the west.

The huge desolation of the marshes stretched away to the horizon and the border of the desert. Bitterns stood by the stagnant pools and jackals skulked through the low bushes; but there was no sign of the caravan of the wise men, far or near.

At the edge of the terrace he saw a little cairn of broken bricks, and under them a piece of parchment. He caught it up and read: "We have waited past the midnight, and can delay no longer. We go to find the King. Follow us across the desert."

Artaban sat down upon the

ground and covered his head in despair.

"How can I cross the desert," said he, "with no food and with a spent horse? I must return to Babylon, sell my sapphire, and buy a train of camels, and provision for the journey. I may never overtake my friends. Only God the merciful knows whether I shall not lose the sight of the King because I tarried to show mercy."

For the
Sake of
a Little
Child

There was a silence in the Hall of Dreams, where I was listening to the story of the Other Wise Man. And through this silence I saw, but very dimly, his figure passing over the dreary undulations of the desert, high upon the back of his camel, rocking steadily onward like a ship over the waves.

The land of death spread its cruel net around him. The stony wastes bore no fruit but briers and thorns. The dark ledges of rock thrust themselves above the surface here and there, like the bones of perished monsters. Arid and inhospitable mountain ranges rose before him, furrowed with dry channels of ancient torrents, white and ghastly as scars on the face of nature. Shifting hills of treacherous sand were heaped like tombs along the horizon. By day, the fierce heat pressed its intolerable burden on the quivering air; and no living creature moved on the dumb, swooning earth, but tiny jerboas scuttling through the parched bushes, or lizards vanishing in the clefts of the rock. By night the jackals prowled and barked in the distance, and the lion made the black ravines echo with his hollow roaring, while a bitter blighting chill followed the fever of the day. Through heat and cold, the Magian moved steadily onward.

Then I saw the gardens and orchards of Damascus, watered by the streams of Abana and Pharpar with their sloping swards inlaid with bloom, and their thickets of myrrh and roses. I saw also the long, snowy ridge of Hermon, and the dark groves of cedars, and the

valley of the Jordan, and the blue
waters of the Lake of Galilee, and
the fertile plain of Esdraelon, and
the hills of Ephraim, and the high-
lands of Judah. Through all these
I followed the figure of Artaban
moving steadily onward, until he
arrived at Bethlehem. And it
was the third day after the three
wise men had come to that place
and had found Mary and Joseph,
with the young child, Jesus, and
had laid their gifts of gold and
frankincense and myrrh at his feet.

Then the other wise man drew
near, weary, but full of hope, bear-
ing his ruby and his pearl to offer
to the King. "For now at last,"
he said, "I shall surely find him,
though it be alone, and later than
my brethren. This is the place of
which the Hebrew exile told me
that the prophets had spoken, and

here I shall behold the rising of the great light. But I must inquire about the visit of my brethren, and to what house the star directed them, and to whom they presented their tribute."

The streets of the village seemed to be deserted, and Artaban wondered whether the men had all gone up to the hill-pastures to bring down their sheep. From the open door of a low stone cottage he heard the sound of a woman's voice singing softly. He entered and found a young mother hushing her baby to rest. She told him of the strangers from the far East who had appeared in the village three days ago, and how they said that a star had guided them to the place where Joseph of Nazareth was lodging with his wife and her new-born child, and how they had paid reverence to the child and given him many rich gifts.

"But the travellers disappeared again," she continued, "as suddenly as they had come. We were afraid at the strangeness of their visit. We could not understand it. The man of Nazareth took the babe and his mother and fled away that same night secretly, and it was whispered that they were going far away to Egypt. Ever since, there has been a spell upon the village; something evil hangs over it. They say that the Roman soldiers are coming from Jerusalem to force a new tax from us, and the men have driven the flocks and herds far back among the hills, and hidden themselves to escape it."

Artaban listened to her gentle,

timid speech, and the child in her arms looked up in his face and smiled, stretching out its rosy hands to grasp at the winged circle of gold on his breast. His heart warmed to the touch. It seemed like a greeting of love and trust to one who had journeyed long in loneliness and perplexity, fighting with his own doubts and fears, and following a light that was veiled in clouds.

"Might not this child have been the promised Prince?" he asked within himself, as he touched its soft cheek. "Kings have been borne ere now in lowlier houses than this, and the favourite of the stars may rise even from a cottage. But it has not seemed good to the God of Wisdom to reward my search so soon and so easily. The one whom I seek has gone before me; and now I must follow the King to Egypt."

The young mother laid the babe in its cradle, and rose to minister to the wants of the strange guest that fate had brought into her house. She set food before him, the plain fare of peasants, but willingly offered, and therefore full of refreshment for the soul as well as for the body. Artaban accepted it gratefully; and, as he ate, the child fell into a happy slumber, and murmured sweetly in its dreams, and a great peace filled the quiet room.

But suddenly there came the noise of a wild confusion and uproar in the streets of the village, a shrieking and wailing of women's voices, a clangour of brazen trumpets and a clashing of swords, and a desperate cry: "The soldiers!

the soldiers of Herod! They are killing our children."

The young mother's face grew white with terror. She clasped her child to her bosom, and crouched motionless in the darkest corner of the room, covering him with the folds of her robe, lest he should wake and cry.

But Artaban went quickly and stood in the doorway of the house. His broad shoulders filled the portal from side to side, and the peak of his white cap all but touched the lintel.

The soldiers came hurrying down the street with bloody hands and dripping swords. At the sight of the stranger in his imposing dress they hesitated with surprise. The captain of the band approached the threshold to thrust him aside. But Artaban did not stir. His face was as calm as though he were watching the stars, and in his eyes there burned that steady radiance before which even the half-tamed hunting leopard shrinks and the fierce blood-hound pauses in his leap. He held the soldier silently for an instant, and then said in a low voice:

"I am all alone in this place, and I am waiting to give this jewel to the prudent captain who will leave me in peace."

He showed the ruby, glistening in the hollow of his hand like a great drop of blood.

The captain was amazed at the splendour of the gem. The pupils of his eyes expanded with desire, and the hard lines of greed wrinkled around his lips. He stretched out his hand and took the ruby.

"March on!" he cried to his men,

"there is no child here. The house is still."

The clamour and the clang of arms passed down the street as the headlong fury of the chase sweeps by the secret covert where the trembling deer is hidden. Artaban re-entered the cottage. He turned his face to the east and prayed:

"God of truth, forgive my sin! I have said the thing that is not, to save the life of a child. And two of my gifts are gone. I have spent for man that which was meant for God. Shall I ever be worthy to see the face of the King?"

But the voice of the woman, weeping for joy in the shadow behind him, said very gently:

"Because thou hast saved the life of my little one, may the Lord bless thee and keep thee; the Lord make His face to shine upon thee and be gracious unto thee; the Lord lift up His countenance upon thee and give thee peace."

In the
Hidden Way
of Sorrow

*T*hen again there was a silence in the Hall of Dreams, deeper and more mysterious than the first interval, and I understood that the years of Artaban were flowing very swiftly under the stillness of that clinging fog, and I caught only a glimpse, here and there, of the river of his life shining through the shadows that concealed its course.

I saw him moving among the throngs of men in populous Egypt, seeking everywhere for traces of the household that had come down from Bethlehem, and finding them under the spreading sycamore-trees of Heliopolis, and beneath the walls of the Roman fortress of New Babylon beside the Nile—traces so faint and dim that they vanished before him continually, as footprints on the hard river-sand glisten for a moment with moisture and then disappear.

I saw him again at the foot of the pyramids, which lifted their sharp points into the intense saffron glow of the sunset sky, changeless monuments of the perishable glory and the imperishable hope of man. He looked up into the vast countenance of the crouching Sphinx, and vainly tried to read the meaning of the calm eyes and smiling mouth. Was it, indeed, the mockery of all effort and all aspiration, as Tigranes had said—the cruel jest of a riddle that has no answer, a search that never can succeed? Or was there a touch of pity and encouragement in that inscrutable smile—a promise that even the defeated should attain a victory, and the disappointed should discover a prize, and the ignorant should be made wise, and the blind should see, and the wandering should come into the haven at last?

I saw him again in an obscure house of Alexandria, taking counsel with a Hebrew rabbi. The venerable man, bending over the rolls of parchment on which the prophecies of Israel were written, read aloud the pathetic words which foretold the sufferings of the promised Messiah—the despised and rejected of men, the man of sorrows and the acquaintance of grief.

"And remember, my son," said he, fixing his deep-set eyes upon the face of Artaban, "the King whom you are seeking is not to be found in a palace, nor among the rich and powerful. If the light of the world and the glory of Israel had been appointed to come with the greatness of earthly splendour, it must have appeared long ago. For no son of Abraham will ever again rival the power which Joseph had in the palaces of Egypt, or the magnificence of Solomon throned between the lions in Jerusalem. But the light for which the world is waiting is a new light, the glory that shall rise out of patient and triumphant suffering. And the kingdom which is to be established forever is a new kingdom, the royalty of perfect and unconquerable love.

"I do not know how this shall come to pass, nor how the turbulent kings and peoples of earth shall be brought to acknowledge the Messiah and pay homage to Him. But this I know. Those who seek Him will do well to look among the poor and the lowly, the sorrowful and the oppressed."

So I saw the other wise man again and again, travelling from place to place, and searching among the people of the dispersion, with whom the little family from Bethlehem might, perhaps, have found a refuge. He passed through countries where famine lay heavy upon the land and the poor were crying for bread. He made his dwelling in plague-stricken cities where the sick were languishing in the bitter companionship of helpless misery. He visited the oppressed and the afflicted in the gloom of subterranean prisons, and the crowded wretchedness of slave-markets, and the weary toil of galley-ships. In all this populous and intricate world of anguish, though he found none to worship, he found many to help. He fed the hungry, and clothed the naked, and healed the sick, and comforted the captive; and his years went by more swiftly than the weaver's shuttle that flashes back and forth through the loom while the web grows and the invisible pattern is completed.

It seemed almost as if he had forgotten his quest. But once I saw him for a moment as he stood alone at sunrise, waiting at the gate of a Roman prison. He had taken from a secret resting-place in his bosom the pearl, the last of his jewels. As he looked at it, a mellower lustre, a soft and irides-cent light, full of shifting gleams of azure and rose, trembled upon its surface. It seemed to have absor-bed some reflection of the colours of the lost sapphire and ruby. So the profound, secret purpose of a noble life draws into itself the

memories of past joy and past
sorrow. All that has helped it, all
that has hindered it, is transfused
by a subtle magic into its very es-
sence. It becomes more luminous
and precious the longer it is carried close to the warmth of the
beating heart.

Then, at last, while I was think-
ing of this pearl, and of its meaning, I heard the end of the story
of the Other Wise Man.

A
Pearl
of Great
Price

$\mathcal{T}$hree-and-thirty years of the life of Artaban had passed, and he was still a pilgrim, and a seeker after light. His hair, once darker than the cliffs of Zagros, was now white as the wintry snow that covered them. His eyes, that once flashed like flames of fire, were dull as embers smouldering among the ashes.

Worn and weary and ready to die, but still looking for the King, he had come for the last time to Jerusalem. He had often visited the holy city before, and had searched through all its lanes and crowded hovels and black prisons without finding any trace of the family of Nazarenes who had fled from Bethlehem long ago. But now it seemed as if he must make one more effort, and something whispered in his heart that, at last, he might succeed.

It was the season of the Passover. The city was thronged with strangers. The children of Israel, scattered in far lands all over the world, had returned to the Temple for the great feast, and there had been a confusion of tongues in the narrow streets for many days.

But on this day there was a singular agitation visible in the multitude. The sky was veiled with a portentous gloom, and currents of excitement seemed to flash through the crowd like the thrill which shakes the forest on the eve of a storm. A secret tide was sweeping them all one way. The clatter of sandals, and the soft, thick sound of thousands of bare feet shuffling over the stones, flowed unceasingly along the street that leads to the Damascus gate.

Artaban joined company with a group of people from his own country, Parthian Jews who had come up to keep the Passover, and inquired of them the cause of the tumult, and where they were going.

"We are going," they answered, "to the place called Golgotha, outside the city walls, where there is to be an execution. Have you not heard what has happened? Two famous robbers are to be crucified, and with them another, called Jesus of Nazareth, a man who has done many wonderful works among the people, so that they love him greatly. But the priests and elders have said that he must die, because he gave himself out to be the Son of God. And Pilate has sent him to the cross because he said that he was the 'King of the Jews'."

How strangely these familiar words fell upon the tired heart of Artaban! They had led him for a lifetime over land and sea. And now they came to him darkly and mysteriously like a message of despair. The King had arisen, but He had been denied and cast out. He was about to perish. Perhaps He was already dying. Could it be the same who had been born in Bethlehem thirty-three years ago, at whose birth the star had appeared in heaven, and of whose coming the prophets had spoken?

Artaban's heart beat unsteadily with that troubled, doubtful apprehension which is the excitement of old age. But he said within himself: "The ways of God are stranger than the thoughts of men, and it may be that I shall find the King, at last, in the hands of His enemies, and shall come in time to offer my pearl for his ransom before He dies."

So the old man followed the multitude with slow and painful steps toward the Damascus gate of the city. Just beyond the entrance of the guard-house a troop of Macedonian soldiers came down the street, dragging a young girl with torn dress and dishevelled hair. As the Magian paused to look at her with compassion, she broke suddenly from the hands of her tormentors and threw herself at his feet, clasping him around the knees. She had seen his white cap and the winged circle on his breast.

"Have pity on me," she cried, "and save me, for the sake of the God of purity! I also am a daugh-

ter of the true religion which is
taught by the Magi. My father
was a merchant of Parthia, but he
is dead, and I am seized for his
debts to be sold as a slave. Save
me from worse than death.''

Artaban trembled.

It was the old conflict in his
soul, which had come to him in
the palm-grove of Babylon and in
the cottage at Bethlehem—the
conflict between the expectation
of faith and the impulse of love.
Twice the gift which he had con-
secrated to the worship of religion
had been drawn from his hand to
the service of humanity. This
was the third trial, the ultimate
probation, the final and irrevocable
choice.

Was it his great opportunity or
his last temptation? He could not
tell. One thing only was clear in

the darkness of his mind—it was inevitable. And does not the inevitable come from God?

One thing only was sure to his divided heart—to rescue this helpless girl would be a true deed of love. And is not love the light of the soul?

He took the pearl from his bosom. Never had it seemed so luminous, so radiant, so full of tender, living lustre. He laid it in the hand of the slave.

"This is thy ransom, daughter! It is the last of my treasures which I kept for the King."

While he spoke the darkness of the sky thickened, and shuddering tremors ran through the earth, heaving convulsively like the breast of one who struggles with mighty grief.

The walls of the houses rocked to and fro. Stones were loosened and crashed into the street. Dust clouds filled the air. The soldiers fled in terror, reeling like drunken men. But Artaban and the girl whom he had ransomed crouched helpless beneath the wall of the Praetorium.

What had he to fear? What had he to live for? He had given away the last remnant of his tribute for the King. He had parted with the last hope of finding Him. The quest was over, and it had failed. But even in that thought, accepted and embraced, there was peace. It was not resignation. It was not submission. It was something more profound and searching. He knew that all was well, because he had done the best that he could, from day to day. He had been true to the light that had been given to him. He had looked for more. And if he had not found it, if a failure was all that came out of his life, doubtless that was the best that was possible. He had not seen the revelation of "life everlasting, incorruptible and immortal". But he knew that even if he could live his earthly life over again, it could not be otherwise than it had been.

One more lingering pulsation of the earthquake quivered through the ground. A heavy tile, shaken from the roof, fell and struck the old man on the temple. He lay breathless and pale, with his grey head resting on the young girl's shoulder, and the blood trickling from the wound. As she bent over him, fearing that he was dead, there came a voice through the twilight, very small and still, like music sounding from a distance, in which the notes are clear but the words are lost. The girl turned to see if some one had spoken from the window above them, but she saw no one.

Then the old man's lips began to move, as if in answer, and she heard him say in the Parthian tongue:

"Not so, my Lord: For when saw I thee an-hungered and fed thee? Or thirsty, and gave thee drink? When saw I thee a stranger, and took thee in? Or naked, and clothed thee? When saw I thee sick or in prison, and came unto thee? Three-and-thirty years have I looked for thee; but I have never seen thy face, nor ministered to thee, my King."

He ceased, and the sweet voice came again. And again the maid heard it, very faintly and far away. But now it seemed as though she understood the words:

"Verily I say unto thee, Inasmuch as thou hast done it unto one of the least of these my brethren, thou hast done it unto me."

A calm radiance of wonder and joy lighted the pale face of Artaban like the first ray of dawn on a snowy mountain-peak. One long, last breath of relief exhaled gently from his lips.

His journey was ended. His treasures were accepted. The Other Wise Man had found the King.